Adelaide

Zara Jenkins

DEDICATION

Mommy for being there for me every day (The trip to Vail was lovely.)

CONTENTS

ACKNOWLEDGMENTS

My mother for making this book possible and for inspiring me. My family for encouragement, support, and love.

1 THE OLD HOTEL

It was a dark and misty night at Vail Mountain and almost everything in the city was closed. A woman named Eliza and her daughter, Adelaide, were stranded among the streets of Vail Mountain's darkest parts. Unsure of where to go, they had caught the glimpse of an old hotel. The rumor was that this very hotel was most known for all of its cobwebs and piles of dust, but somehow its quality was very highly rated. As the girl and her mother approached the center of the village, suddenly there was an unexpected black-out. In the dark, scared and cold, they marched along while the sound of their boots crunched against the snow. This movement had awakened the birds who were sleeping in the trees, surrounding the city. As the birds flapped their wings wildly, Adelaide started to look around. She then noticed that despite the blackout, the lights of the old hotel were on--so it probably was still open. The sight grew clearer, but there was a tall gate was preventing Adelaide and her mother from entering the building. The lobby of the hotel, Vail Manor, was the first thing they saw when they tried to look through the openings of the gate. The mother walked closer to the big gate, clutching her daughter tightly on the shoulders; her heart beating out of her chest. When they came in con-tact with the gate, it detected Adelaide and her mother. Finally, the gate slowly opened with a loud, screeching sound. The birds flew over, and rested on the top of the rusty gate, staring at the girl and the woman who were shivering the entire time. As they passed the entrance slowly, the birds cocked their heads in confusion, seemingly wondering who these people were and what they were doing here. The girl, who was holding her mother's hand, was scared, but when they walked inside Vail Manor, the attendant at the front desk, Michelle, made her feel more comfortable. She had a bright, welcoming smile which made her appear easier to trust. Michelle escorted Adelaide and her mother across the hall, to the first room, nothing special. And the best part was that it was free (there was a promotion where the first night is free for first-time guests). They were hoping to find a place to eat after they settled in, but there weren't many places that were open anyway. So, they decided just to eat in the morning. They looked out the window, gazing back at the glowing mountains that were covered in beautiful, white snow. Adelaide and her mother dozed off, falling fast asleep. The birds remained outside the window, still peering at the mother and girl from the trees.

2 THE RESTAURANT MANAGER

It was a foggy morning and the birds were awake as well as Adelaide and Eliza. Adelaide and her mother went out for a walk in the city to get to know the area and figure out where to eat, but as they roamed the streets, they spotted a burned-down restaurant in the distance. The birds stopped chirping and joined the couple, perching them-selves on an electrical wire nearby. Adelaide, who was suddenly walking faster, was curious of an old-looking business manager who was placing caution tape on the windows and doors of the restaurant. She began to scrape her shoes against the pavement, pacing towards the man. The sun began to melt the snow slowly and Adelaide's mother was get-ting tired of chasing her. The girl finally got an image of the manager's face through the fog. Then, Adelaide faded into the mist where Eliza could not see her child. After a little bit, Adelaide's mother caught up to her breathing deeply after each step she took. They had stopped to take a good look at the man who had stared back. "Why, hello there! Where might you two young ladies be going at a time like this?" the man smiled. "Hello. We are just taking a walk around this beautiful town. We couldn't help admiring your hard work. My daughter and I must have been interested. Sorry for bothering you, sir and, well, we'll be moving on. Nice meeting you. Oh, and do you happen to know a restaurant nearby?" "Why, yes indeed Madame. May I recommend you go across the street to Sprouts. Their food it delicious!" the manager exclaimed. "Okay, we'll take a look. Thank you very much, sir!" Her mother replied. "Please, call me, Gerald," the man-ager begged. "Good day, Gerald. Hope to see you again!" "Wait, Miss! Have you ever been to Vail? You don't look familiar." Gerald made a confused face. "Well no. We stopped by hoping to find a place to stay. "Come on, Adelaide, You must be starving!" her mother assumed. They walked alongside the road and passed many old antique shops, but then they were interrupted by a big grocery store that towered right in front of them, taller than the other locations next door. It was made of brick, engraved with pictures of green, healthy foods. They walked inside and browsed for a while. The woman and her beloved child were tempted by the stocked goods, so they had grabbed a few items off the shelves. They ravished each fruit they bought, from licking the fresh straw-berries, to peeling the ripe bananas. They nibbled until there was nothing left to devour. They left with their leftovers, heading back to their hotel.

3 ADELAIDE'S NEW DAYCARE

On the way to the hotel, they noticed a daycare that had just opened up recently. Adelaide's mother decided to sign Adelaide up, so she had something to do while her mother explored Vail. It's a struggle and quite tiring to keep track of a 7-year old girl as adventurous as Adelaide. The little girl wasn't big about the idea, but at least she would make some friends during her experience--hopefully. As her mother walked out into the fog, Adelaide waved in the distance, her nose pressing against the cold, glass window. The lady at the front desk told her to go to the ladybugs room. Adelaide slowly walked through the hallway passing other classes. She soon found the "Ladybug's" classroom, and entered the space, stumbling over the toys that were blocking the door. Adelaide froze: The thought of everybody staring at her was quite embarrassing. The girl bit her lip, took a big gulp, and soft steps towards a group of children. She counted 6 girls and one elderly-looking woman wearing a pink apron, who was distributing food to the children. Written on their name tags were Ellie, Katie, Jenni, Fiona, Lilliana, and Rebecca. Katie introduced herself first. "Hi. I like your hair. I like everyone's hair. Mine is short and ugly and curly and--I don't think it's

5

ugly." Rebecca also commented, interrupting Katie abruptly. Then the woman spoke up. "Oh, are you, Adelaide, the new ladybug? "Y-yes," she replied nervously. "Oh wonderful. We have hamburgers, peas, mashed potatoes, and if you want any brownies come tell me, okay?" she said happily. Her name was Ms. Chenille. Ms. Chenille pulled out a chair in between Jenni and Lilliana. Lilliana was kind of mean, so she didn't want to talk to Adelaide. She turned to her friend Fiona. Jenni tapped Adelaide on the shoulder, happy to talk to Adelaide because she had no friends to speak of. "Hi! Ms. Chenille told us about you. You're the new ladybug. I'm Jenni. What's your name?" Jenni asked calmly. "I'm Adelaide. Yes, I'm the new ladybug. So, is it time for lunch?" "Yeah, it lunchtime, she's passing it out. After lunch, it'll be recess," Jenni explained. "Wanna be friends?" Adelaide asked, feeling less embarrassed. "Sure," said Jenni. Everyone began to eat their hamburgers, poking the mashed potatoes with plastic spoons, peas slipping off their spoons--plopping on the floor continuously in a sloppy pattern. Suddenly, Lilliana fell out of her chair, placing the blame on Adelaide. She was shocked: This already, on her first day! At first it was quiet, messy lunch time, but now everything has changed. When Ms. Chenille was finished cleaning up most of the peas that fell on the floor she spotted Adelaide and Lilliana arguing. Adelaide had a feeling that Lilliana and herself weren't going to be friends any time soon. But at least she could hang out with Jenni...

4 BACK TO THE HOTEL

Adelaide's mother ventured throughout most of the city, now with a better sense of what it had to offer. She picked up Adelaide from the Vail Mountain Tiny Town, Adelaide's daycare. They walked down the street into the cold air, still not used to the birds making their horrible sounds. The sky began to dim and the day grew darker. As Adelaide and her mother got closer and closer to Vail Manor, each and every step they took drew them closer to the darkness. At one point, the mist gathered, hovering in the spot were Adelaide and her mother stood. Not knowing where they were or where they should go, they were lost in the foggy streets, stuck with only the sound of the creepy birds and complete darkness. It took a while until some of the fog cleared, and when it calmed down, Adelaide and her mother could see the birds perched atop the gate again. She knew the hotel was nearby, so the girl and her mother walked in determination to the entrance of Vail Manor. As a matter of fact, they were two blocks away from the hotel. Adelaide could almost see the city's lights going out, one by one, as the fog piled up into bunches again. Finally, Adelaide and her mother could spot the hotel's silhouette easier. They were standing in front of the only thing that lit up: the lamppost, which flickered about every 3 seconds and made a buzzing sound. After passing another store-front, they found themselves in the dirt and gravel, somehow managing to reach the slightly visible hotel. Looking back towards the street and seeing the birds circling for food, Adelaide noticed the restaurant manager walking past the frightening gate with a sad look on his face. He placed a note in between the openings of the gate, and then continued walking off into the mist where Adelaide couldn't see him anymore. Feeling curious, she was determined to find out about the note. She walked inside with her mother, dragging her by the hand into the room, and falling asleep within minutes.

5 THE MANAGER'S MESSAGE

There lay Adelaide, yawning as she pulled back the red velvet covers to the guest bed. Her mother had opened the blinds, allowing the window to light up the shadowy corners of the room. Adelaide couldn't wait to see Jenni again, but she hadn't forgotten about the note that Gerald left behind. Adelaide noticed her mother dozing off on the edge of the bed, exhausted from last night. As the girl watched her mother slip into a temporary hibernation, Adelaide slid the guest room card into her pocket and peeked out of the door into the lobby. No one was there. She quietly tip-toed into the hall, looking both ways as if she were crossing the street. The wooden floor creaked as Adelaide took big, loud steps farther away from the guest room. Then she heard a voice from the front desk. The attendant was talking in her sleep. The lights were off, but the room was bright, so the girl knew what to do. She exited the building and started down the path, feeling the wetness soak into her bunny slippers like a sponge collecting water. The gate now was only a few feet away, she could manage the grossness of the water. Adelaide arrived at the entrance of the gate, her slippers far from dry. She took the note (that had been wrapped with some kind of expensive fabric). It was slightly damp at the corners, but the little girl had tiny fingers to grab the envelope without tearing it. She peeked in-side, and began to read the message. Adelaide heard wagon wheels rolling on the stoned path. She ran back towards Vail Manor, annoyed and determined as her soaked slippers made a squishy noise along with the sound of the wheels- both sounds increasing, making her worried that her mother may have been awakened by the disturbance. The girl happened to be breathing deeply as she raced to the guest room, slamming the door be-hind her. She was relieved to see her sleeping mother still resting. But not for long. Adelaide's mother heard the slam of the door and shot up, startled as if someone had banged a drum right next her ears. Rattled, her dear mother looked at Adelaide as if she had broken her favorite vase. Then there was the look. The one you get when your child thinks they didn't do anything wrong, but on the inside, they know they did. The puppy-dog eyes wouldn't work on mom today. So Adelaide stood there, until her mother spoke up in a rather grim voice, "What were you thinking wandering outside on your own?!" the girl shrugged, exposing the note in her hand. "What's that? In your hand... Mail? For us? Why? Is that even ours? Adelaide!" It was hard to answer her furious mother, but she knew she had to admit the truth. "Mommy, I found this paper in the gate's cracks and I-I don't know why it was there, how I found it there or who left it there, but all I know is that I was curious of it being there, that's all..." Adelaide mumbled the lie into the neckline of her collar, her breath visible in the cold air and her cheeks on fire since from stretching the truth. She didn't even wanna hear the consequences that were upon herself. "Well, darling don't leave the hotel room without letting me know, m-kay?" Her mother smiled mildly with her hand on her hips. "Yes ma'am," Adelaide sighed with relief. "Let's take you to Tiny Town, okay pumpkin? I'm sure they'll serve you a yummy breakfast today," her

ADELAIDE

mother replied in a soft, calming voice.

6 LILLIANA'S BIRTHDAY PARTY

Adelaide had reached the daycare just in time for pancakes with syrup and bacon. She definitely didn't plan on eating it combined together like Katie did. The energetic child kissed her mother and walked inside. Jenni waved when she saw her friend walk into the room. Ms. Chenille also realized Adelaide had arrived, and brushed off some white powder from her apron. (It sort of looked like flour from the pancakes). "Hello, Adelaide! We have a seat right here next to Jenni and Rebecca. There's a plate waiting for you right here! Okay Ladybugs, let's eat!" She exclaimed, dusting off another white patch of flour from her apron. After almost everyone had eaten all their food, Lilliana and Fiona popped out their seats with pink cards in their hands. "Everybody is invited to my special birthday party on Friday!" Lilliana shouted in excitement. "That's three days from now, so be prepared to eat some cake!" Fiona added. Fiona sat back down in the seat across from Adelaide and Jenni, who weren't as excited. Lilliana grinned back with a fake smile that was, of course, meant for Jenni and her new best friend. Katie started to jump up and down, and Ellie and Rebecca danced their way to the trash can where everyone dumped their leftovers. Mostly tiny pieces of bacon were scraped of off the girls' plates and tossed in the trash. Ms. Chenille wasn't fond of this behavior, but she wanted her girls to have fun, so she told everyone there was a surprise in the playroom for all Ladybugs. The Grasshoppers beat them to it. "Hello, Mrs. Shannon. I see you're all playing ladybug games." Ms. Chenille was bothered by the fact that the Grasshoppers were messing up the Ladybugs' surprise. "Why, yes indeed we are, Ms. Chenille. We all know sharing is caring, so of course it's ok to borrow your equipment? Right, Ms. Chenille?" Ms. Shannon laughed, clicking her heels on the slippery floor, inching closer to Ms. Chenille and her Ladybugs. Ellie stood in front of Ms. Shannon, suddenly staring up at her with a look of sadness. "This is ours! We are using it! So, Give it back! Did you know it's Lilliana's birthday? Her ultimate desire would be if we could use it really quick," Ellie blurted anxiously. Lilliana nodded in agreement. Ms. Shannon gave Ellie a hard look, bent down to her level and stared. She raised her pointy nails slowly up to Ellie face. "Well, a birthday of Lilliana's eh? Without us Grasshoppers? Well, where's the cake!" Ms. Shannon chuckled and lightly tapped Ellie on the nose and stood back up. The ladybugs frowned in anger. "We were hoping that you could let us celebrate. Alone. Right now. Without you. And the Grasshoppers. Oh, and leave the equipment. Thank you, Ms. Shannon." Ms. Chenille spoke deeply. "Now out you go," she said as she motioned for Ms. Shannon and her children to leave. "Sorry about that Ladybugs. Now who's ready to have some fun!" the instructor exclaimed. She hoped everyone would forget about that little scene with Ms. Shannon. "Don't worry. Us Grasshoppers always get our way..." Ms. Shannon snarled, peering into the playroom. The corners of her mouth formed into a sneaky smile.

7 THE RECESS MASSACRE

Everyone had fun during the party, but it was time for recess. The Grasshoppers were also heading to recess at the same time as the Ladybugs. The Butterflies and Caterpillars left recess 5 minutes prior, but the Fireflies had just left. The schedule all fell together, but the lady at the front desk never felt appreciated. Ms. Chenille had an idea to fix this problem. "Ladybugs! Come here real quick! So guys, you all know the woman at the front office of Vail Mountain's Sunnyside Daycare, Mrs. Sonya? Well, she doesn't feel very appreciated, so after recess we are going to make her cards. That's all. M-kay? You can all play now. Have fun!" The Ladybugs spread out, all around the playground. Jenni and Adelaide headed over to the monkey bars, but there was a bundle of other little kids occupying the area. The Grasshoppers! They were mad at the Ladybugs for taking the equipment and not sharing, so they hijacked the monkey bars and wouldn't share those. Revenge is what they wanted. Now this made the Ladybugs furious. "Hey, no fair! It's our turn to use the monkey bars, and you're hogging them," said Adelaide. Lilliana, Katie, Ellie, Rebecca, Jenni and Fiona agreed with Adelaide. She was standing up for the Ladybugs. "We're sorry, but we're also using it," a little boy replied as he dismounted. "I'm Jeremy and I really need a favor. Go Away!" he yelled, getting back onto the monkey bars. "We hope you fall off, Jeremy," Rebecca cried as she stuck her tongue out at him. "Yeah, and we hope you don't get hurt," Lilliana added sarcastically. Fiona made a face, trying to mock the boy. The ladybugs walked away. Fiona stayed at the monkey bars, watching the Grasshoppers with narrowed eyes and crossed arms. Katie and Ellie decided headed for the swings. Three of out of the four swings were isolated from the Ladybugs, and apparently, they were being used by the Grasshoppers. "Wait... Weren't you at the monkey bars? Jeremy, please get off!" Katie wasn't happy about what she observed. "Sorry, but I just got on so...finders keepers, losers weepers." Jeremy seemed to be everywhere. "That's it! I'm pushing you off." Katie could tell Ellie wasn't happy either. Ellie walked over to Jeremy's swing as he moved his eyes, following her steps while Katie placed her hands on her hips and pursed her lips. Katie was practically distracting Jeremy from Ellie, who happened to be slowly approaching with her palms towards his back, motioning for Katie to taunt Jeremy. He became quite angry. He stopped watching Katie. At the perfect moment, she gently shoved him off of the swing. Now, focusing on the teacher's reaction, Katie pulled Ellie away, without drawing attention to themselves. They were probably not concerned if Jeremy was okay. They joined the other ladybugs. Jeremy rattled to Ms. Shannon, who cocked her head and leaned over him. "Those Ladybugs have quite some nerve. I've got my eyes laid on that Katie girl." Jeremy then pointed to Adelaide. "Ah, that new girl. She and her friend Jenni are the ones I like the most....so far." Ms. Shannon sighed.

☐

8 THE FAMOUS GUEST IN TOWN

Rumor was that a special visitor was about to arrive to Vail the next day. Adelaide had a lot on her mind. She honestly didn't even care about this world-renowned guest. She wondered: Had her daycare gone to war? Well, with things this wild, the girl didn't want to know what it'll be like tomorrow. After a long sleep, Adelaide learned the visitor, Diane Springs, had arrived. Diane was a famous actress who came to see "Vail Mountain History". It was all over the town, on TV Commercials, and in the newspapers. The event finally caught Adelaide's attention. "Who was this mysterious star?" she thought to herself. "And why would she decide to come to a place as old as this?" It was believed that Diane was actually born in Vail. The Springs house was burnt a couple of days after her 5th birthday. Her family also left her a young age. All the actress had was her mother. She had this in common with Adelaide. People thought Diane just missed her hometown, and that she wanted to visit. Others believed that since it was close to her birthday, Diane just wanted to see the gravestones of her ancestors. Diane and her mother, Trisha, used to walk the alleys of Vail's deepest parts and ventured into the most beautiful places in the city. Until, a couple years later, a storm destroyed part of the town. Unfortunately, Diane's mother was caught in this storm and died. The girl was only 19. Diane saved enough money to move from her job at Vail's daycare to start her life in Las Vegas. She never wanted to see Vail again. Now that she's returned, she was apparently staying in the same hotel as Adelaide. Diane had arrived at the spooky hotel around the time that Adelaide was eating breakfast with her mother. Upon seeing the girl and her, Diane sighed. She had a feeling she would have to introduce herself, just to be polite. Adelaide slowly turned her head and calmly took a deep breath. Her mother spoke first and exclaimed

"Oh, hi. You must be Diane! Everyone's been talking about you." Diane felt at ease. "Oh hi! Yes, I am Diane. May I ask who you might be?" she replied. "I'm Eliza and this is Adelaide. So, why are you back in Vail?" Adelaide's mother inquired. "You know? I thought no one remembered my story, I mean, it was so long ago," Diane shrugged. "Well, almost everybody knows what amazing obstacles you faced! Oh, look at the time, I must be going. Nice meeting you, Ms. Springs," Eliza chuckled. As Adelaide and her mother walked out, Diane went back to her room and saw something out of the window. She hates when people call her Ms. Springs.

9 THE SECRET NOTE

Diane opened the window; she thought it may have been a bird, but the figure she saw was something that looked like paper. Diane peered over the ledge and tried to reach it. Her fingers barely brushed the folded note, but she managed to grab it. Diane had so many questions--she didn't know if it was meant for her, she didn't know who it was from, nor why it was there.
She grasped the note, put on some clothes and
strolled around for a while. She looked at the note and pondered who might've given it to her. She went to the bakery at Sprout. She just couldn't figure out who gave her the note. She sat on the bench right outside of the store, and opened the note and read ten simple words:

> Please visit us at the
> Vail Mountain Daycare!
>
> -Thank you -- Ms. Springs!

So, Diane walked to the daycare.
Surprisingly, she ran into Adelaide. This daycare is the same one Diane went to as little girl. Ever since she heard

Diane's past, Adelaide was scared that something would happen to her own mother.

Diane stayed with Adelaide until her friend, Jenni, showed up. "Hey, Adelaide right? Who are you waiting for?" she asked. "My best friend, Jenni. I never go inside without her," the little girl answered. "Hmm.. And why is that?" Diane inquired. "She's my best friend and we do everything together. Hey, what's that in your hand?" Diane opened her hand. "Um.. just some piece of paper. Do you know who it's from?" Diane mumbled.

"Oh, I gave it to you. Yesterday at daycare, Jenni and I wanted to get to know you, so we were wondering if you would come to the daycare. So can you come again tomorrow?" Adelaide begged. "Okay, I will," Diane responded. "Yay! Wow, Jenni sure is late," Adelaide whined. "I'm sure she's fine, just some quick hold up. I'll be right back, Adelaide." Diane smiled. She then went inside to use the restroom in the daycare--leaving Adelaide worried and all by herself.

10 THE FRIENDSHIP BRACELETS

Finally, Jenni showed up. "Hey Adelaide. Whoa! Diane Springs is actually here! I thought they were joking!" Jenni gasped. They all walked in the ladybugs classroom. "Hi, Jenni. Hello, Adelaide. Well, Ms. Springs! We're pleased to have you come to our class. Come and sit, girls," Ms. Chenille gulped. The two girls sat down. "Oh, thank you. Ooh: Arts and crafts!"

Diane sat next to the group. They were making jewelry. "I'm making a bracelet," Adelaide smiled. "So am I!" exclaimed Jenni. "Hey, let's make friendship bracelets, so we can always remember each other!" They cheered.

"That's a great idea! I want mine to be pink, green, and purple," Adelaide beamed. "I'm using blue, pink, and yellow on my bracelet," Jenni answered happily. So they made their bracelets, and when they were done, they put them. Even 'til this very day, they never ever ever ever ever take their bracelets off. When they eat, take showers, go to sleep, wake up, go on fun adventures, they'll look at their bracelets and understand the true meaning of friendship.

Do you have a best friend? If so, the two of you should put these bracelets on, and that'll mean you and your best friend will be best friends. Forever. Just like Adelaide and Jenni.

ABOUT THE AUTHOR

Yes, I'm young (currently 11), but I'm also dedicated and willing to achieve my goals. My passion of writing (realistic fiction) began around age 6. My mother supported my love of writing. We'd listen to audio books in the car and my favorite one was the biography of George Washington Carver. His life story just inspired me to never give up and that's when I decided to make my own story, except I wanted a different genre: realistic fiction. I read a bunch of books for more inspiration, with a desire to become a better writer. I'd practice and study big and strong words for my story, and I did something different. Something unique. Something that was really out there. And hopefully, "Adelaide" inspired you too!

Made in the USA
Columbia, SC
18 June 2020